i A

n T

t I

a S

p N

s P

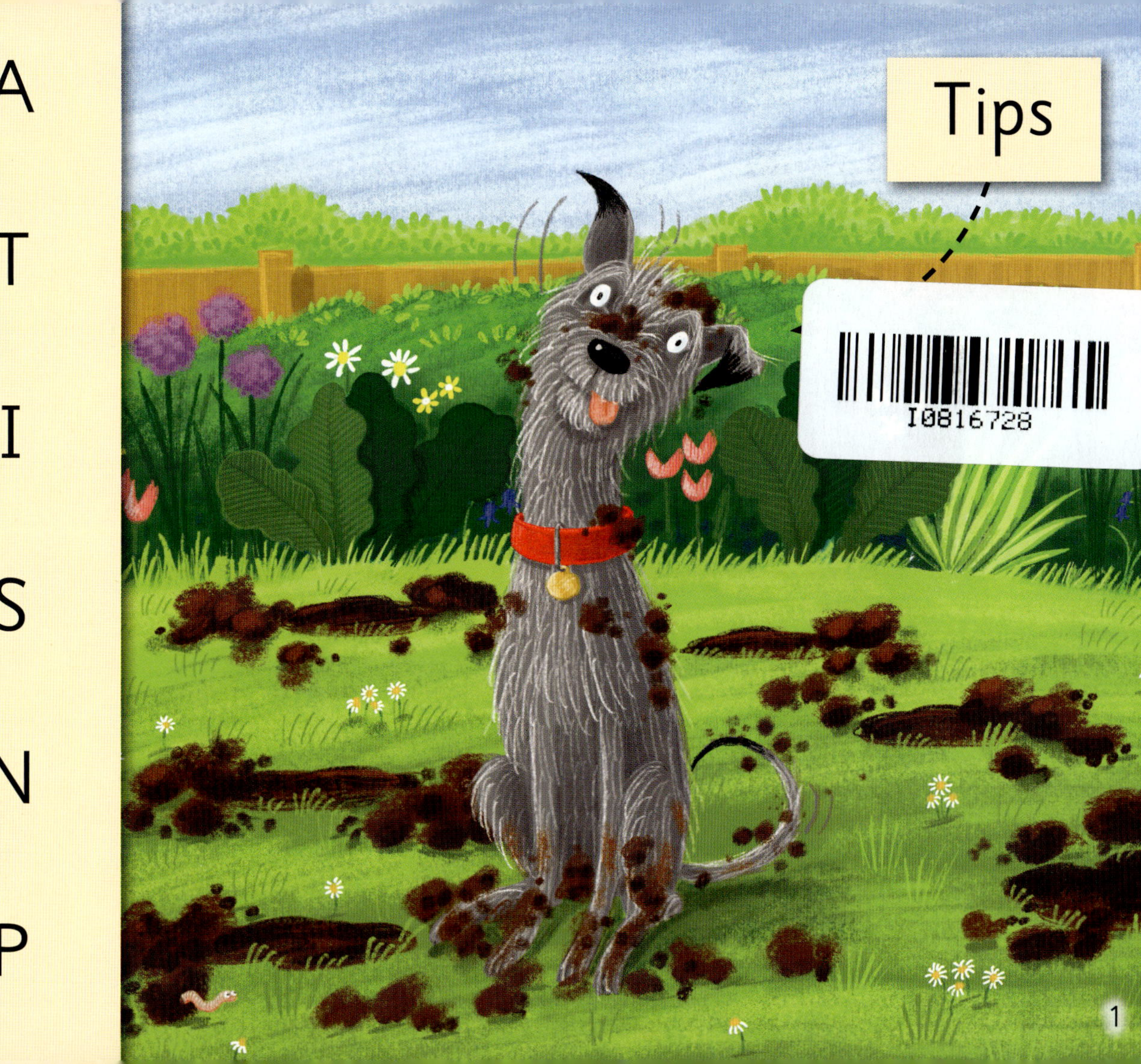

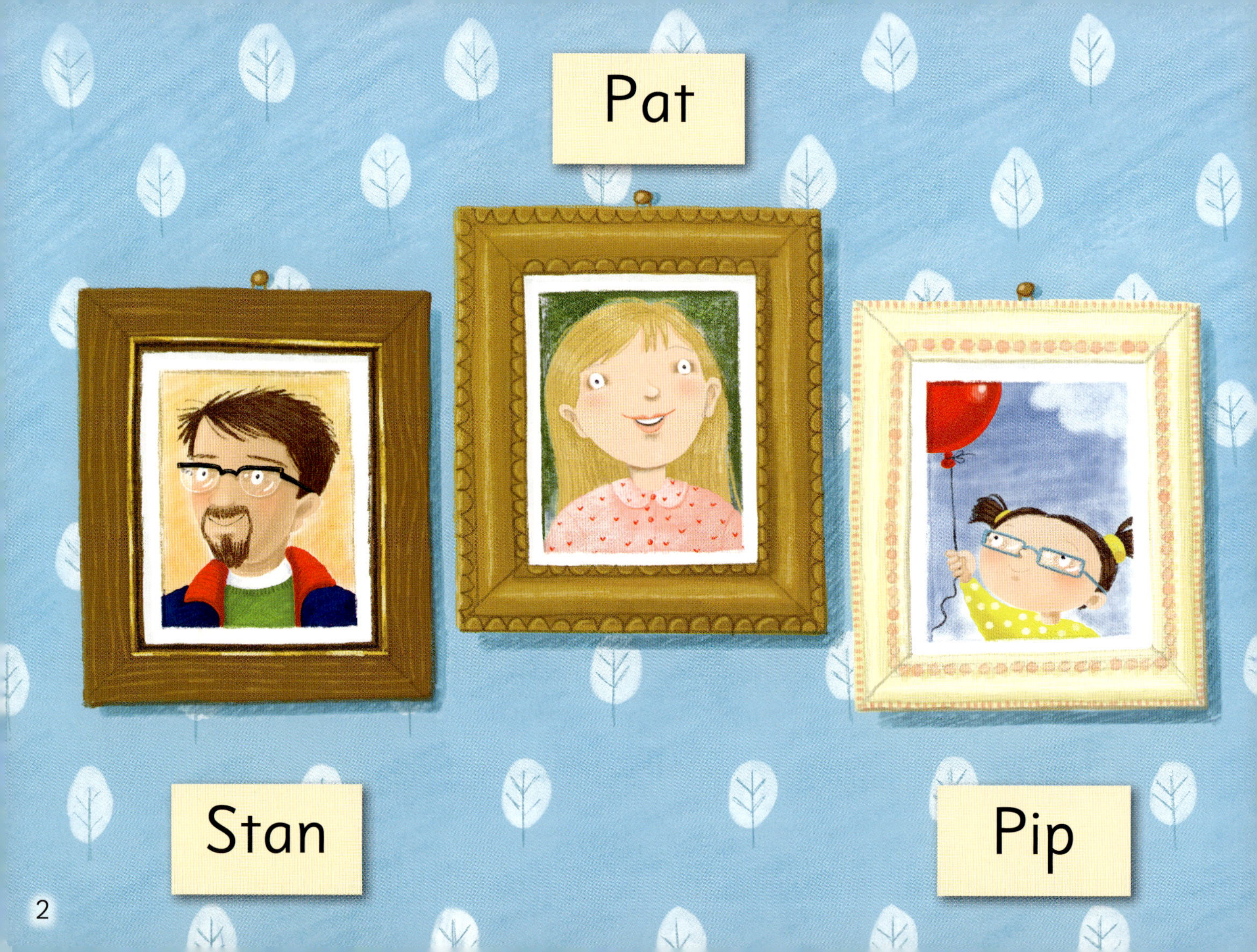
Pat
Stan
Pip

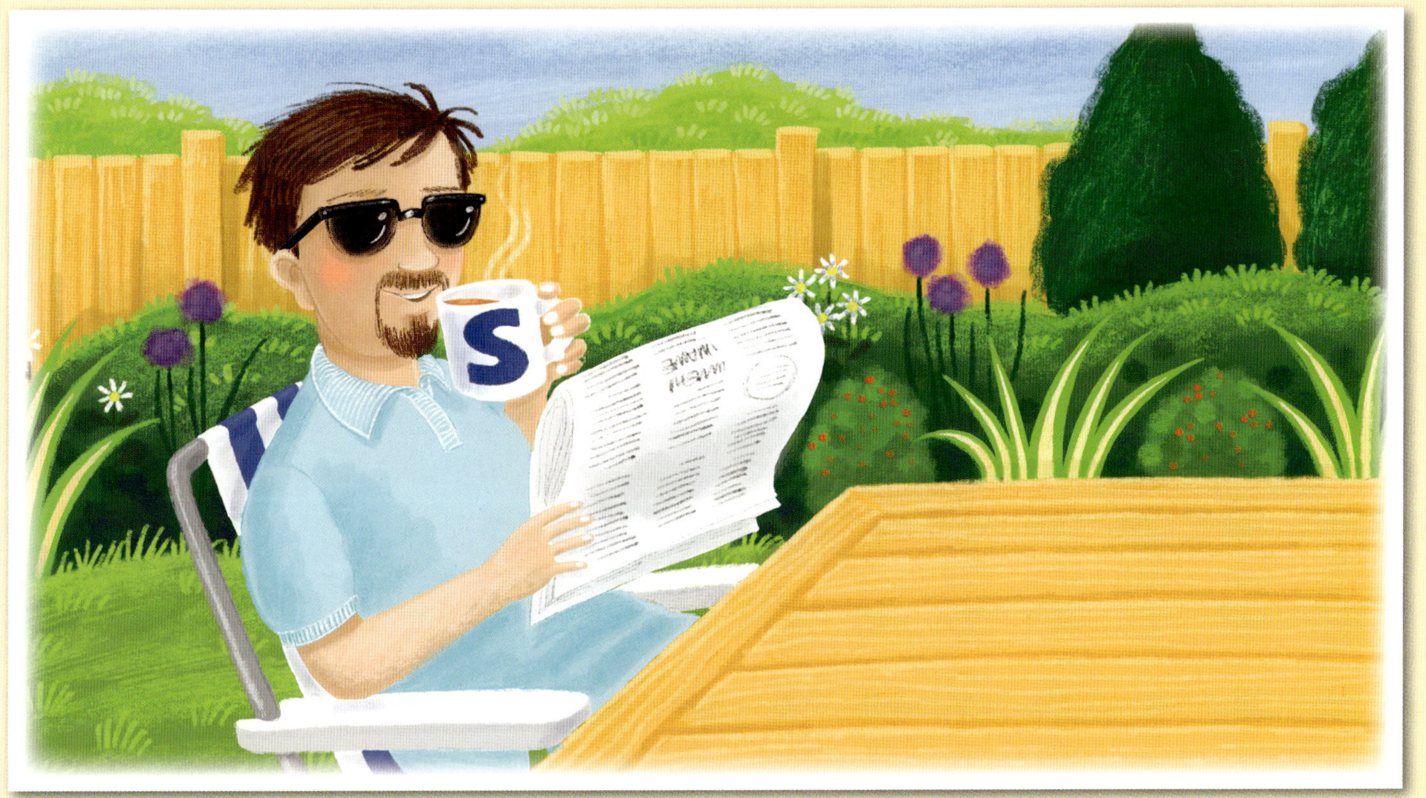

Stan sips.

Pat naps.

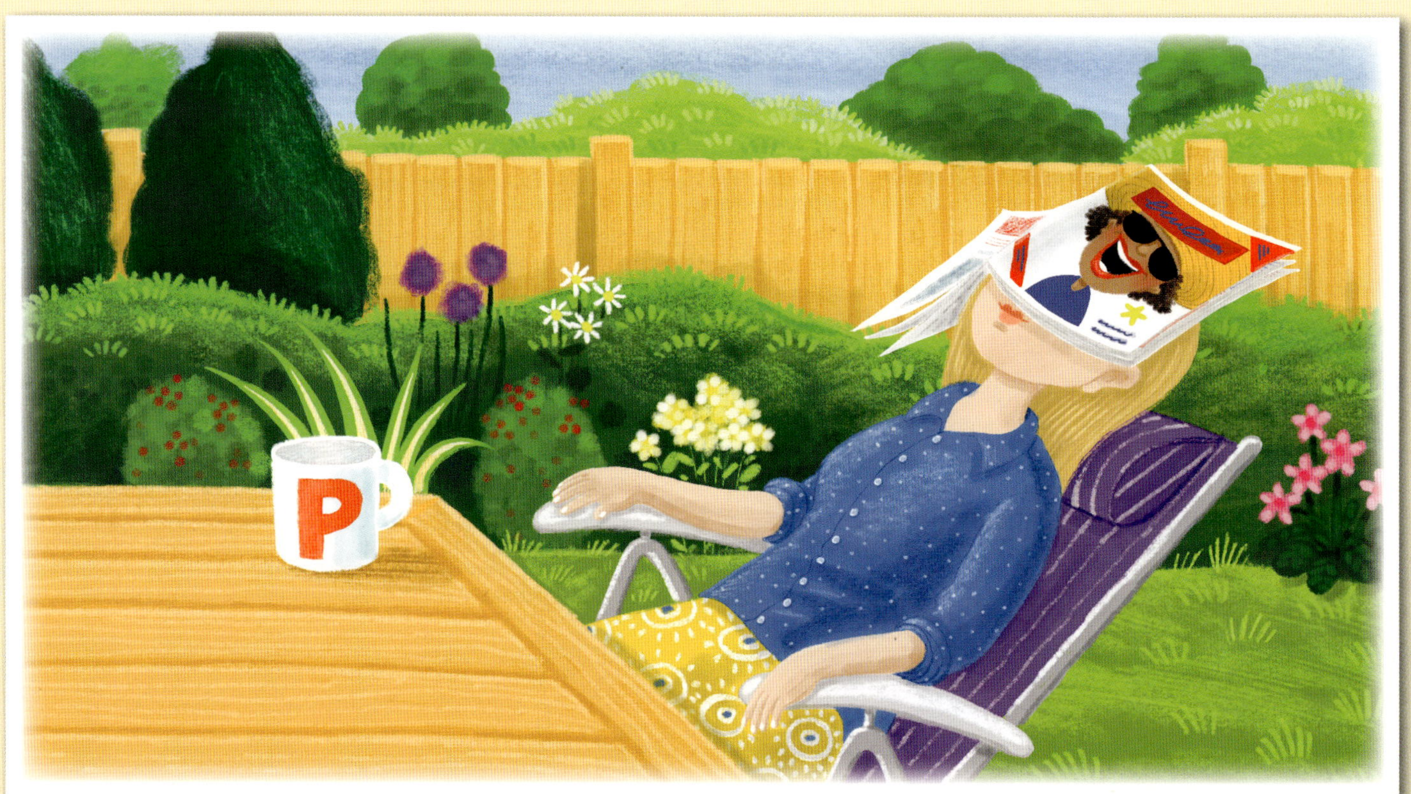

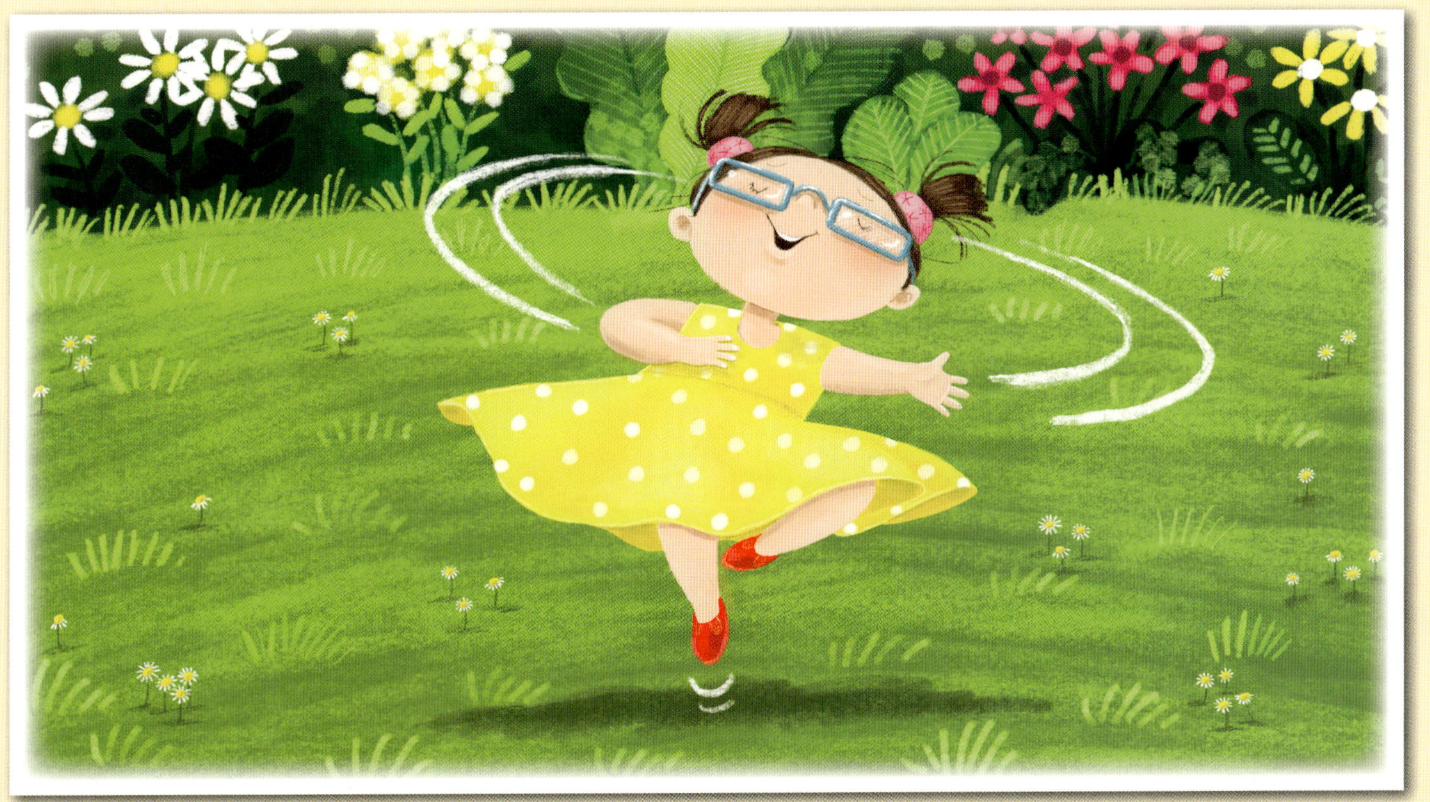

Pip spins.

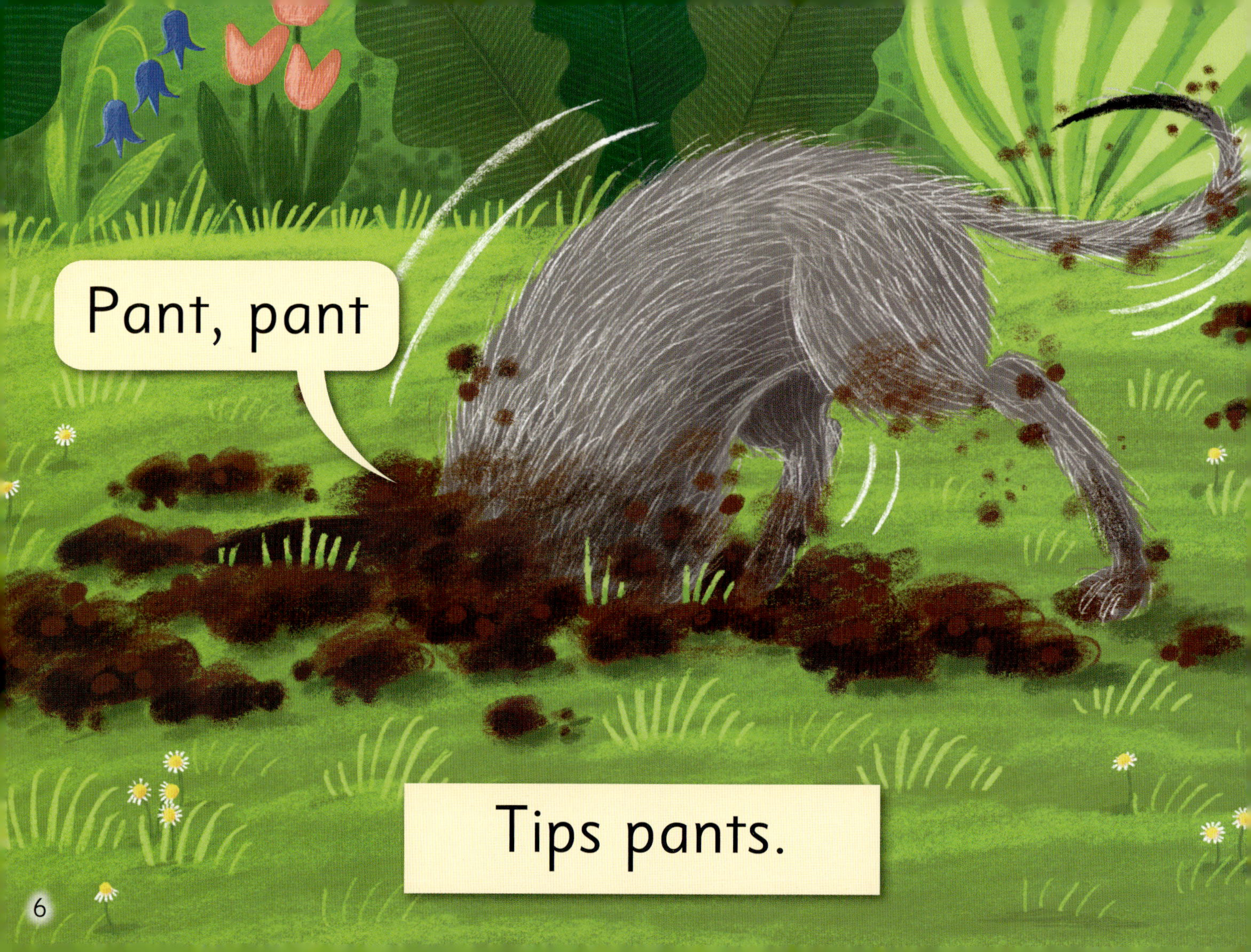

Tips pants.

Tips sits in a pit.

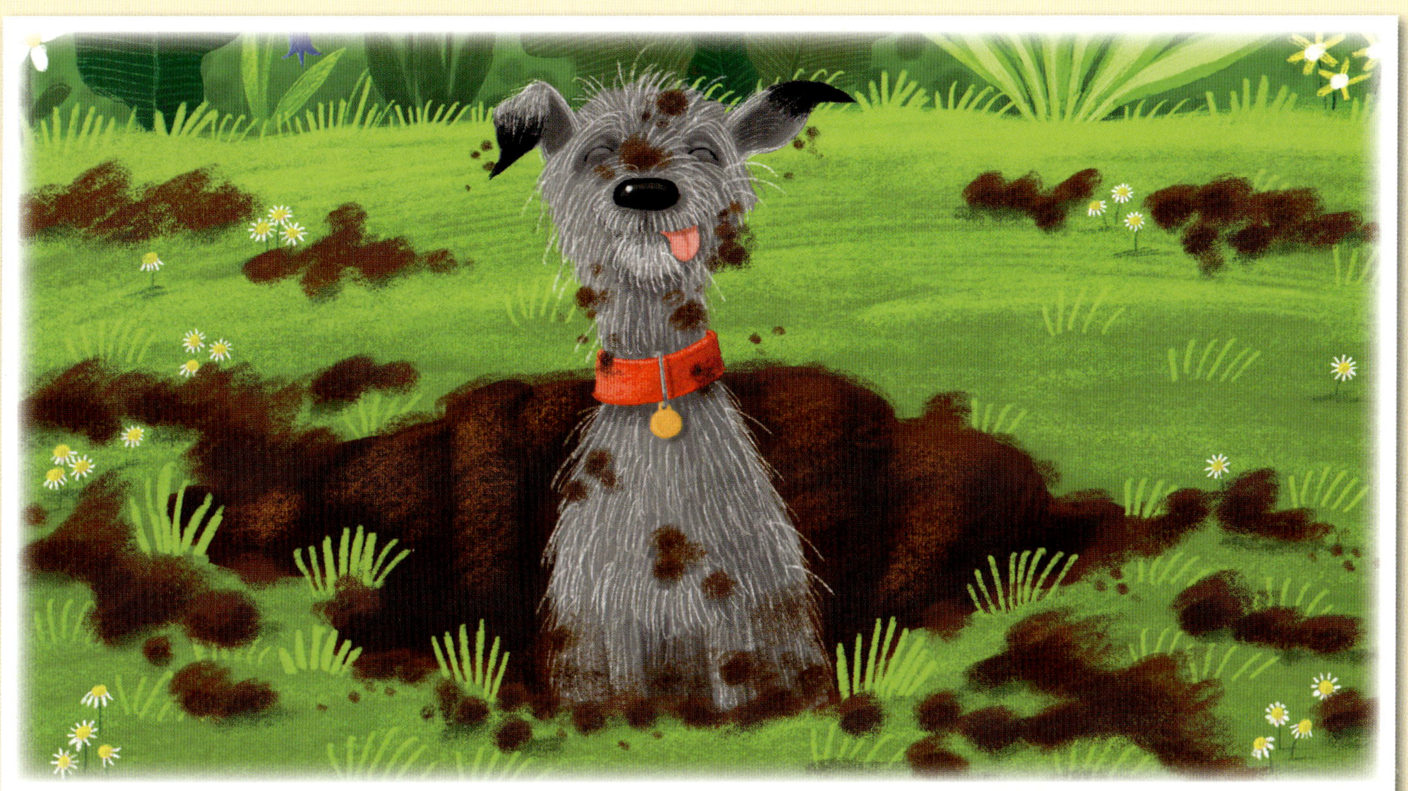

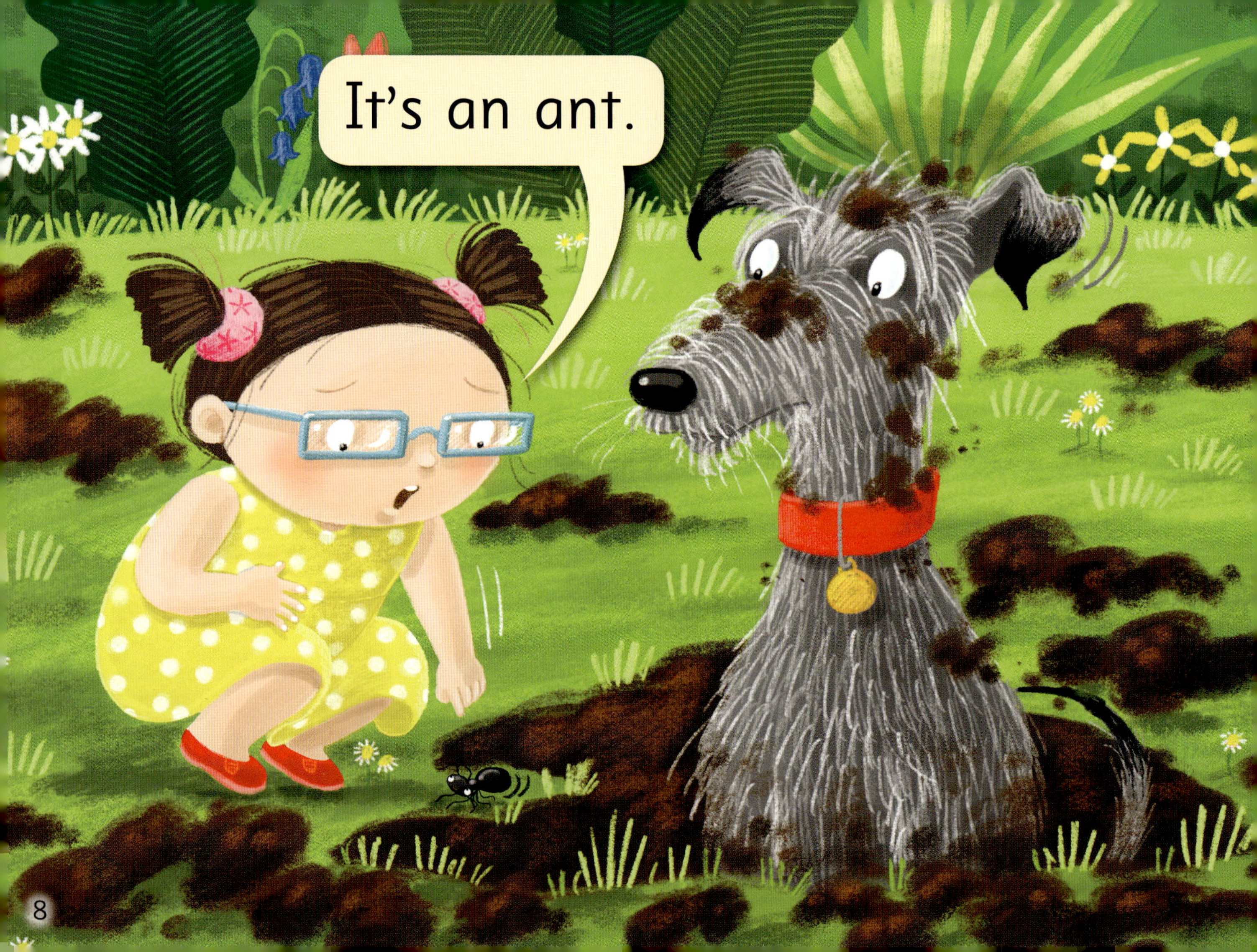
It's an ant.

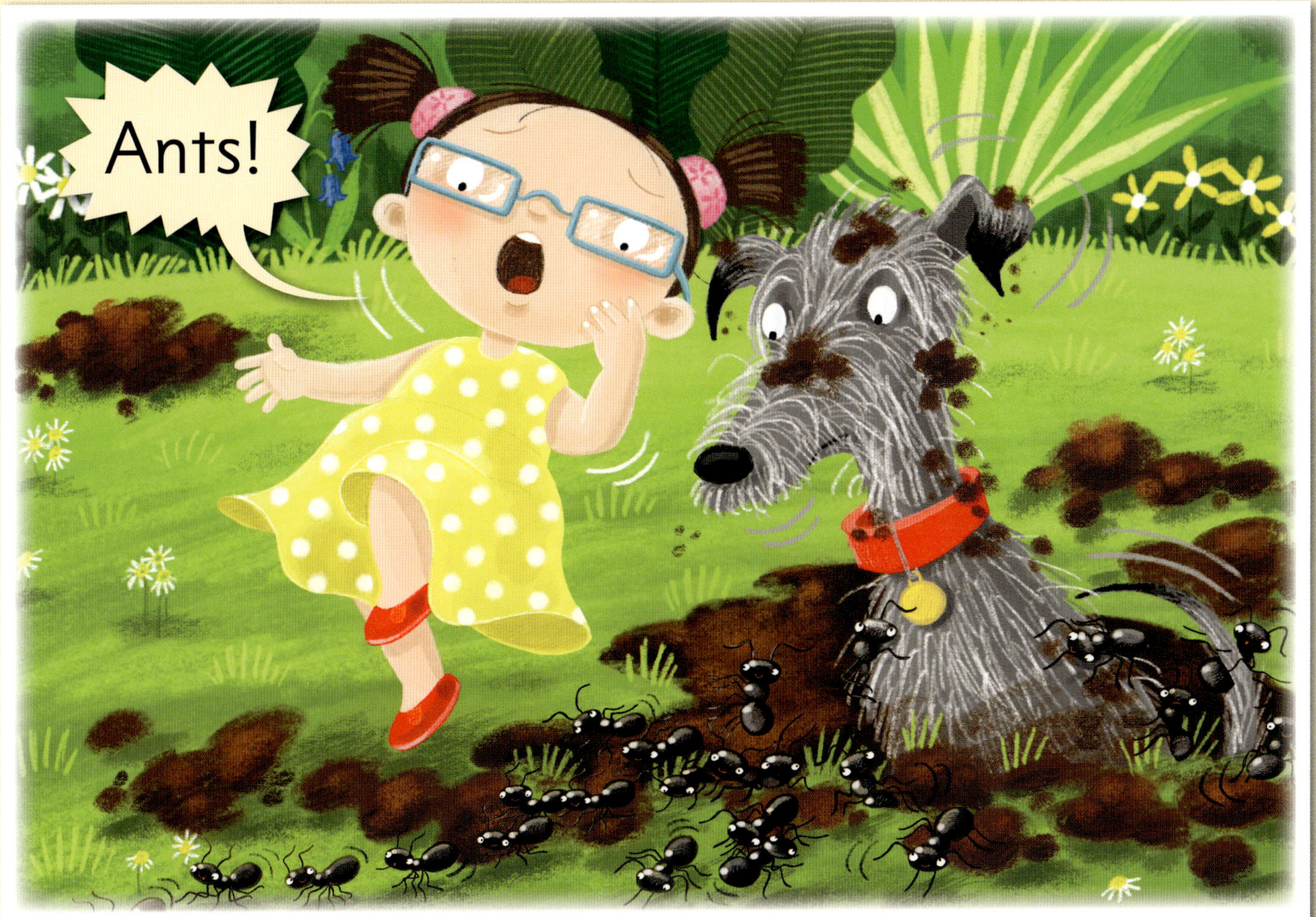
Ants!

Ants nip at Tips.

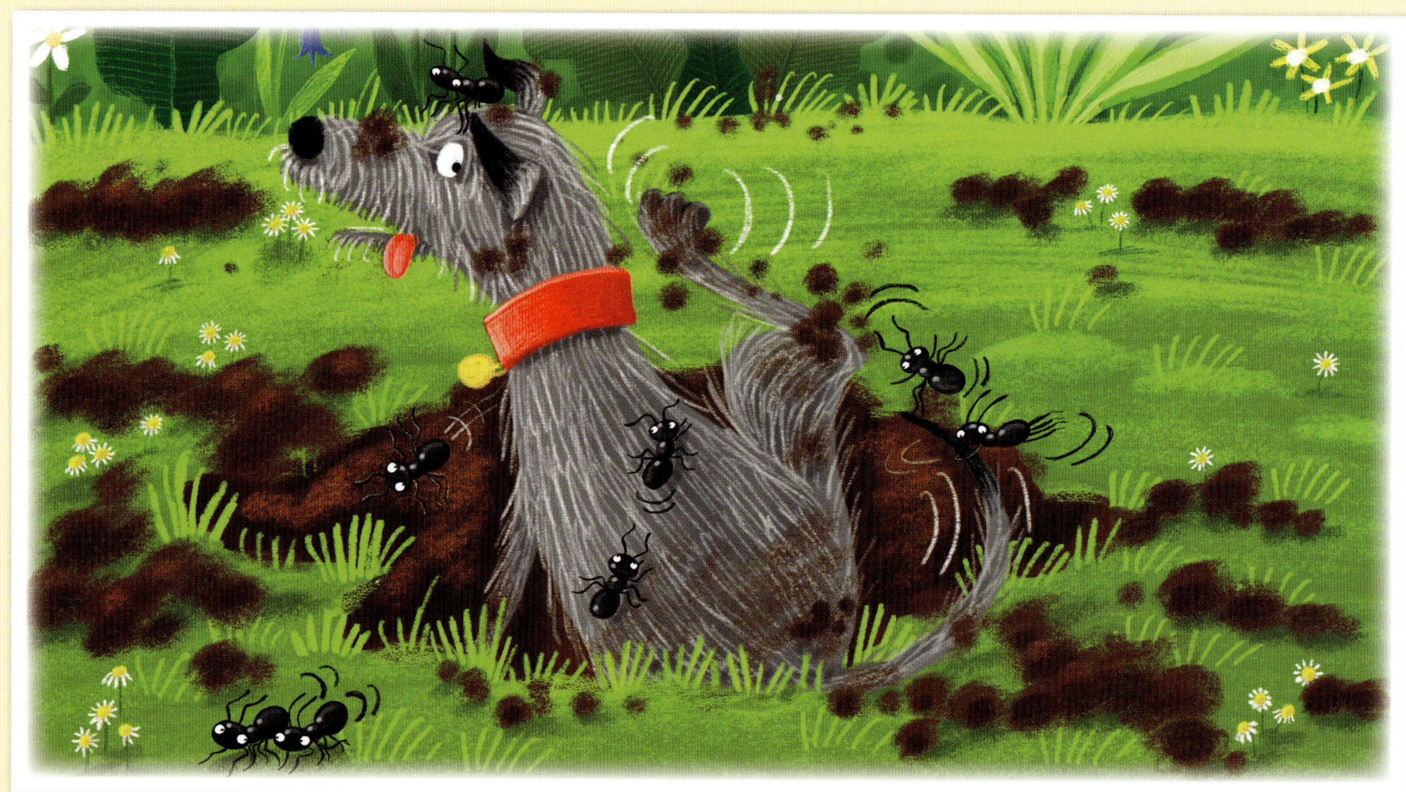

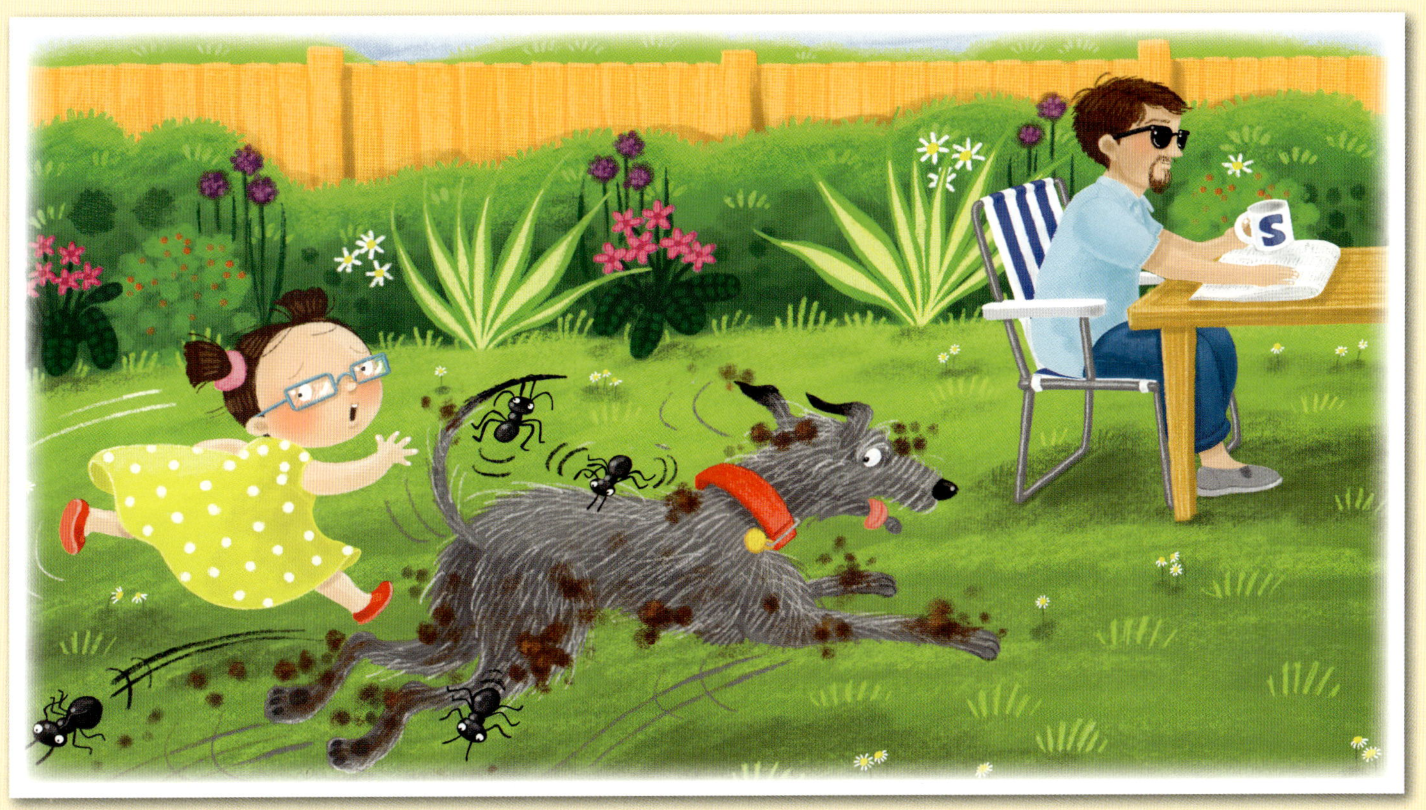

Pant, pant, pant.

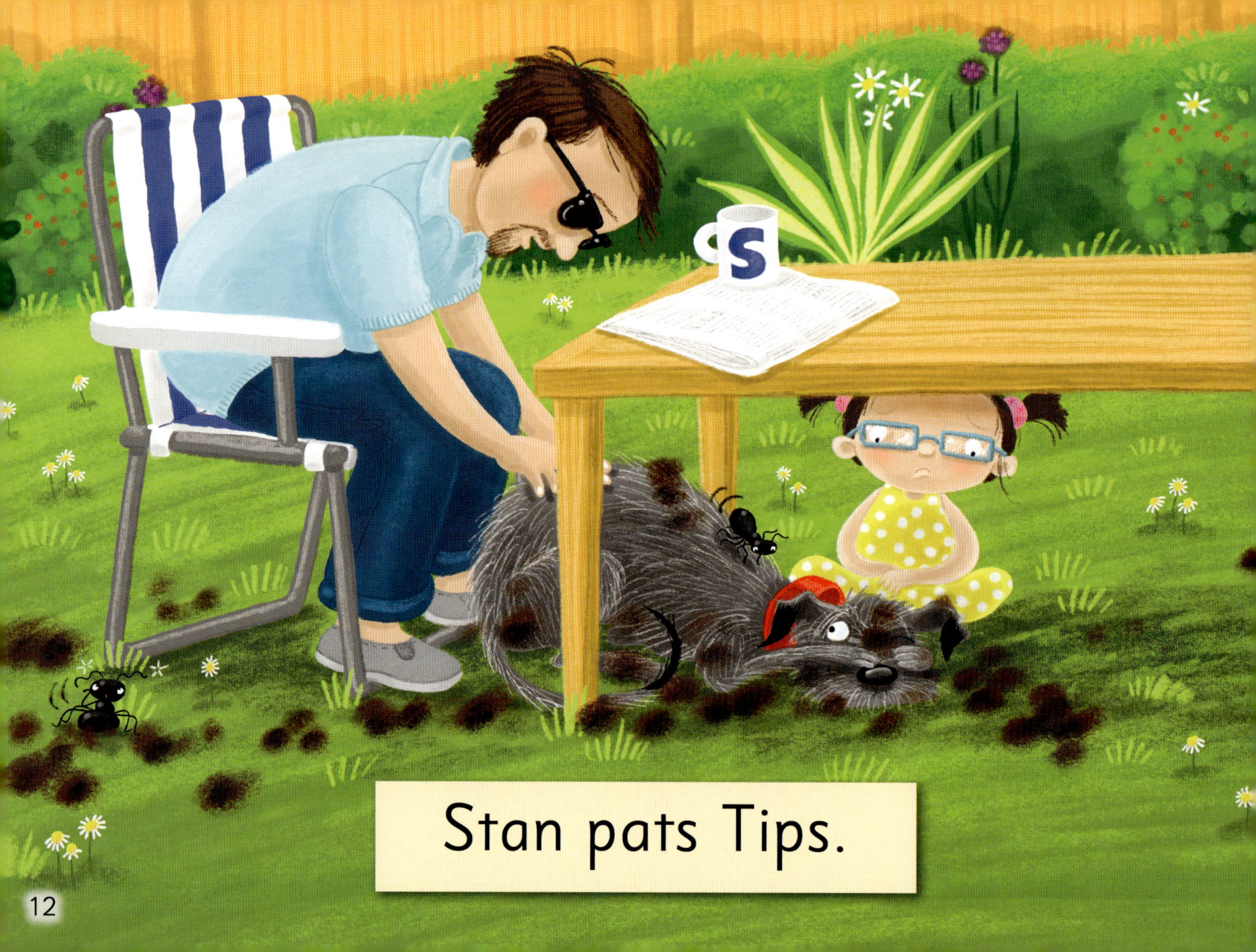
S
Stan pats Tips.